Macarastor

Book One: The Mountain Men

Bob Giel

authorHOUSE®

AuthorHouse™
1663 Liberty Drive
Bloomington, IN 47403
www.authorhouse.com
Phone: 1-800-839-8640

Cover design by Jessica Grassi

First published by AuthorHouse   07/16/2011

ISBN: 978-1-4634-2842-6 (sc)
ISBN: 978-1-4634-2841-9 (ebk)

Printed in the United States of America

This book is printed on acid-free paper.

For Jess and James—
      Who saved my life

For Nancy—
      Who gave me new life

Chapter One

Cason Macara stepped out onto the store's front porch to greet the morning. A tad chilly it was this day but the sun was brightening and it promised warmth. This had become somewhat of a ritual for several weeks now, this stepping out onto the porch to greet the morning. Sure, it was not the morning he was interested in, but the countryside and any activity that might be about. A particular activity, that of a rider approaching would have been a satisfying sight had it presented itself. But this morning held no more hope than did all the others since he began this ridiculous watch.

"Well now," he told himself, "who's to say the man will magically appear as I'm scouring the hills this fine morning? Who's to say he'll appear at all? There was no guarantee, you know. It was a definite 'we'll see what we can do', but, by the saints, that's all it was. Yet here you are, standing here again, looking, waiting. You're daft, don't you know! Get back inside and be about your business!"

Following the order he had just given himself, he slowly turned and took a step toward the door. As his hand went for the latch, something caught his attention. There had been a stirring behind him. He heard nothing and saw nothing, yet he knew that he should turn

1

back around for another look. And so he did, and was presented with the sight, so far in the distance that it was barely visible, of a lone rider leading a pack horse.

"Could it be? Could this be the manifestation of 'we'll see what we can do'?"

He squinted to clear the picture before him but to no avail. There was just too much distance between them even for his keen eyes. He would be forced to wait for the rider to approach before he would know if this were himself, the one he'd asked for.

As he leaned a shoulder against the porch column to wait more comfortably, Macara's thoughts raced back to the beginning of this nightmare.

It was the murder that tore it! Before that, it had just been annoyances, almost pranks, although the loss of anything to the people that lived around the store was serious, they had so little. But, till then, it had been the disappearance of a pig, or a chicken or two. Some lost boots. Others lost rifles.

Then it escalated to horses. Folks began keeping watch. It was the watching that got Will Tremayne. Had he been snug in his cabin that fateful night, enjoying Maggie's fine stew, instead of being camped in the barn waiting for trouble, he'd be with us today. Ah, but the brave boy-o he was would not sit still for being pilfered and so he sat in the dark barn, waiting, when Oren Rudabaugh stepped in, a rope bridle in one hand and a Navy Colt in the other. One could only guess what ensued thereafter, but when Maggie heard the shot splitting the still night, she made a dash outside and saw a dim light coming from the barn.

As she ran toward the barn, the door flew open to reveal a buckskin clad figure up on the mare bareback, with the reins of the rope bridle in hand, brandishing the Colt. Maggie kept coming. She saw no sign of Will and knew he must be in trouble.

The mare bolted at the sight of Maggie and reared a tad, then backed into the barn. As Maggie cleared the threshold of the barn, the rider dug his heels into the horse's flanks and urged her forward. Maggie looked up and, in the light from the lantern on the stall pillar, saw the face of Oren Rudabaugh. Now the horse was making for the door and Rudabaugh was aiming the pistol—at Maggie. She froze for a second, then let out a yelp and threw herself at the hay aside the stall, landing on her face in the stuff.

The great Colt boomed and sent a ball slamming through the barn wall where, a split second before, Maggie had stood. A mad flurry of hooves propelled the mare through the doorway and into the night. Stillness returned to the scene as the sound of the galloping horse disappeared.

Maggie raised her head and began to pull herself up. Her heart was pounding so hard she could almost hear it through her breast. This and the rustling of the hay beneath her held her attention until another sound reached her ears. It was Will and he was calling her name and he was in trouble.

"Will!" she said with alarm.

"Maggie, I'm here. Help me."

She traced the sound of his voice to the stall. As she came around the stall pillar, she saw him, saw her

Will, her love, on his back. The stall was darker and the shadows covered him but she saw him all the same. Her hand went to the lantern and pulled it down. Then she saw the blood on his shirt and she cried out, cried his name and cried out again.

In an instant, she reached him. She set the lantern down and leaned in to cradle him, all the while saying his name, close to hysterical now.

"Maggie, he shot me, shot me bad." His voice was weaker now.

"Don't talk, Will. I'll get help. You'll be fine. You'll see. Cason will fix you right up. You'll be fine." Her voice was comforting and frenetic at the same time.

His hand reached up and touched her arm to stop her ranting.

"Tell Cason. It was Oren Rudabaugh shot me. Tell him." His speech was faint now, raspy.

"I'll tell him, Will. Don't talk. You need your strength. You got to . . ." She stopped short as his head dropped to one side in her lap and the last breath issued loudly from him.

Her hands lifted his head and she found herself shaking him as if to wake him. Her voice called his name more times than she could count each louder than the time before, until it echoed in the stillness of the night. It was then that she allowed herself to admit that her love was gone. In that instant, she realized that she would never again hear him call her name, never again lay with him, never again be his wife. Grief took hold and she sat cradling him and crying hysterically into the night.

Somehow, how she still does not know, but somehow Maggie Tremayne found her way to Macara's place. It was just before dawn when she stepped up onto the porch, the very porch on which he was now standing, and pounded incessantly at the door until Macara, wrapped in a blanket, opened it. She fell into his arms and bawled like a baby.

Calming Maggie took several minutes, at which point Rose Macara poked her eight-year-old head out of the bedroom.

"Da, whatsa matter?" she called sleepily.

"Rose, darling," Macara called back softly, "sure it's nothing for to worry your pretty little head over. Go back to sleep now. There's a fine lass."

The door closed behind Rose. Macara half carried Maggie to the little room in the store he had made into an office and sat her in the desk chair. He made for a lamp and a match and set about eliciting the tale from the still sobbing woman.

"Rudabaugh!" he repeated, when she reached that point in the story that raised the name.

When Maggie finished, he made her as comfortable as possible and got Rose out of bed. Quickly, he got her dressed, put off the answers to her questions, hitched up the buggy and loaded both her and Maggie into it. The trip to the Luce's place took about fifteen minutes at full gallop. When Macara explained himself to Sam and Etta, Etta ushered Rose and Maggie into the Luce cabin. Sam and Macara struck out for the Tremayne homestead.

They found things exactly as Maggie had described them. Carefully, they placed the body of their friend into Macara's buggy for the ride back to the store.

They buried Will the next day. Macara read over him and swore to Maggie that this crime would not go unpunished. Three days later, Macara set out for Denver to seek the help of the law. It would be weeks before he returned with the promise of "we'll see what we can do." He trusted that his gift for convincing would prevail, and, so began the morning watches.

Now, standing on his porch, watching the rider approach, the only thought he could muster was "could it be? Could it be?"

Chapter Two

The beginning of the seventh day on the trail. This was the part of the job Cord liked the least. As much as a goodly sum of his work was done on the trail, the trail was not his favorite place to be. Besides the dust and the dangers of animals and humans lurking about, he mostly disliked the loneliness. Strange that he felt that way, having purposely selected this life of oneness which he led. Maybe it stemmed from his military years and the comrades that fell at his side. Maybe he kept clear of close relationships because the pain of loss was too great to perpetuate. Or maybe it was just the seventh day of this journey and talking to horses had lost its attraction!

As he directed his mount and hauled the reluctant pack animal down the mild grade from the crest of the last hill, his thoughts were changed by the image he perceived in the distance. Looks to be more than just a lodging. That might be the store that was said to be the goal of this trip. Whether to stay or to request directions, Cord was headed straight for the building as he urged the horses from a walk to a lope.

Because this stretch of clearing would take a few minutes to traverse, Cord decided to use the time to go back over the chief's briefing of the case he was about to begin.

There had been a robbery and murder. A farmer had surprised a thief in his barn trying to steal a horse and the farmer took a fatal bullet for his trouble. Cord's orders were to seek out an Irishman named Cason Macara at his store located about midway between Cheyenne and Fort Laramie in the Wyoming Territory. Macara would put him in touch with the only eyewitness to the incident, the farmer's wife. After taking her statement, Cord was to investigate, attempt to locate the assailant, make the arrest and return him to Denver for trial. Unaware of what was to develop, this sounded at the time like a fairly simple task. He would look back on this later and acknowledge the gravity of the situation that he had initially missed.

As he narrowed the distance between himself and the building, Cord saw a figure leaning against the porch post watching him approach. He focused on the man and began to believe that he had reached his goal, that this figure on the porch was indeed Cason Macara.

The man was fairly tall and lean and was dressed in the garb of a lumberjack: black stocking cap, bright plaid shirt and green suspenders supporting blue pin striped britches. His laced boots were knee high, with his pant legs tucked inside them. Flashing out from under the cap was a shock of dark red hair and his face had the ruddy complexion of one quite obviously of Gaelic descent. His face was ruggedly handsome with fine features and bright blue eyes that seemed to possess a smile all their own. He stood proudly and had the clear look of intelligence that had been described to Cord in Denver. As Cord came closer, he became more certain that he had found the man he sought.

Cord reined in at the short hitch rail in front of the porch and struggled with the pack horse to bring the animal alongside. He flashed an embarrassed smile at the man on the porch and the man smiled back, a bright smile that appeared to light up his entire face.

"Good morning." Cord said, "I'm looking for a gent named Cason Macara."

Macara's smile broadened. "Sure, you've found him. That's me."

"Glad to make your acquaintance, sir. Name's Thomas Cord. I'm a U. S. Marshal."

The words changed Macara's demeanor from expectation to elation, his smile to a grin. He leaned away from the post and stepped smartly to the mounted man, his hand outstretched in greeting. Cord leaned over to shake the extended hand and heard Macara's greeting: "It's I that's glad to meet you, me lad. Step down, won't you? Come inside. I've a lot to tell you."

Cord swung down out of the saddle and secured the reins to the rail as Macara seemed to follow his every step. Just then the pack horse bolted slightly and grunted. Quickly, Macara went under the rail and scooped up the animal's reins and lashed them around the rail.

"I'm obliged to you, sir." Cord offered. "That one's a handful at times."

Macara's smile continued. "They all are at times. Now, please, come inside."

Cord followed Macara through the doorway and into the interior of the store. There were the usual stocks of food and work supplies that were the staple of every general store he had ever inhabited. But here things were not strewn about. They were separated and catalogued into shelves and cubbies and in neat stacks around the selling area. Impressive, Cord said to himself and aloud.

Macara turned at the word with a confused look on his face. Cord extended his hand toward the object of his utterance.

"Oh, that." Macara acknowledged. "I've a mite o' time on me hands of late. Business has been slow since Will Tremayne passed. People are sticking close to home."

Cord nodded and continued behind Macara through a heavy curtain into the living quarters. It consisted of a great black stove, some cupboards and a makeshift table and chairs. And, in the far corner stood gingham clad Rose Macara with broom in hand, attempting to sweep some dirt into submission.

"Rose, love," Macara called. Rose turned quickly and flashed a toothy grin in the general direction of the two men. "This is Mr. Cord come to visit." Macara continued and, turning to Cord, completed the introduction: "Here's me pride and joy, sweet Rose she is."

Cord's hand instinctively went to his hat, as one would do in the presence of a lady, but with a flourish, he swept it from his head and took it across his bending body in larger than life bow to the child. "I'm very pleased to make your acquaintance, Miss Rose."

Rose at once giggled and curtsied smartly. "How do you do, Mr. Cord." she said sheepishly.

"I am fine, Miss Rose, the better for having met you this morning."

Rose giggled and curtsied again and was now at a loss for what to say next. She regarded the big man full of trail dust and smiles and instinctively knew that he was a good man, that she was safe in his presence.

Macara moved to Rose and picked her up in his arms. "Now, Rose," he began, "Mr. Cord and I need to have some words together. Now, Mr. Cord has a fine buckskin horse outside that is likely in need of some water. Do you think you could lead him over to the trough for a drink, then hitch him up again?" The girl nodded, "Yes, Da." He lowered her to the floor and she made for the curtain.

"Mind you, now, don't mess with the pack horse. He's a tad skittish, he is."

"Yes, Da." She repeated and disappeared through the curtain.

Macara crossed to the stove and poured out two cups of coffee from the pot that was stationed there. "Now, to the grit of it."

The two men sat at the table across from each other and Macara set about telling the portion of the story that he knew. Cord listened intently but also observed the man as he spoke. His gestures and his gift for the Irish gab aside, Cord sensed the concern that Macara had for the people who lived nearby. He spoke of them as if they were under his charge or that he was in some way responsible for them, for their well being.

Cord had not seen the like of this man before and was impressed by him in a way that he had not known before. Macara was not only father to Rose but felt a parental responsibility for all in the area.

When Macara had finished recounting the incident, Cord allowed that he would need to get the wife's statement down on paper before continuing his investigation.

"Whenever you're ready to go," Macara stated, "I'll take you to her."

"I'm ready now." Cord said as he rose to his feet.

"I'll need to get Rose ready to stay at the Luce's place until we're done. It's not much out of the way to Maggie's."

"Whatever you need to do, sir."

Macara got up with his hands on his hips and a look of fake anger on his face. "Now there you go again! That's got to be at least the fifth time you've 'sirred' me, boy-o. I'll not be asking much of you while you're here, but this I will. Stop calling me sir."

Cord grinned and his hands went up in a gesture of compliance. "As you wish."

Chapter Three

The ride to Sam Luce's place was a quiet one with Cord riding his buckskin and Macara driving the buggy containing Rose and Macara's saddle. Not much could have been discussed owing to the agreement struck by Macara and Cord to shield Rose from knowledge of the Tremayne incident, other than that Will had passed away.

"She'll be growing up soon enough." Macara had offered, "I'll be obliged if she knows no more of this from our talking."

Cord readily agreed, and so silence prevailed.

As the journey progressed, Macara regarded Cord closely. He was intensely interested in this man who exuded such confidence and stature. He observed the way Cord carried himself, straight and proud, both on foot and in the saddle. Cord was a tall man, taller than most, well over six feet he was. And strapping he was. He'd do himself proud in a fight, Macara thought. Not only was he struck by Cord's demeanor, but by his look . . . the cut of his jib, as they had said at sea. Cord was neat and tidy, or as much as a man could be who had just spent a week on the trail. While they were dusty and somewhat wrinkled, his clothes were well kept. He was appropriately garbed in trail clothes, those of a cowhand, but there was some thought behind it. His hat was wide brimmed to ward off the sun and the weather, and he wore chaps over his black pants for protection from brush and branches. His shirt was a dark grey but not well worn, fairly new it was. Tied about his neck was a bright yellow kerchief to absorb the inevitable sweat that the trail generated. But it was the hardware that really caught one's eye, the gun belt and pistol. The belt was beautifully tooled and stitched, and carried probably eighteen to twenty rounds in its bullet loops. There was a scabbard with an ivory handled knife attached to its left side. In the holster, set high on his right hip, with butt situated forward in the manner of carry of the military sat a shiny Smith and Wesson .45 caliber Schofield revolver. This man took pride in his appearance, from his clothes to his well manicured mustache and goatee. He obviously took the time and effort to maintain himself no matter what the circumstances.

The Luce place was not much in the way of prosperity. The small log cabin had been fashioned roughly from the surrounding timberland and Sam's prowess as a carpenter and builder. He had aided Macara in the construction of the store but that structure had been built from a set of plans Macara had acquired from an acquaintance before his arrival in the area. Sam's home, however, had been completely his own creation and erected by his own hand, with Etta's help.

The land was fertile and the Luce's eked out enough to get by on, but they were by no means well off.

But when Will Tremayne and his Maggie arrived to settle, it was Sam who helped them build and get started, and Sam who lent a hand with the clearing and the planting. And it was Sam who, this day, was again at the Tremayne place helping Maggie keep up with it all.

This was apparent to Macara as the buggy approached the cabin and only Etta appeared in the doorway. It was lunch time but Sam was nowhere to be seen.

Etta waived as Macara reined the buggy horse in at the hitch rail and Cord pulled up beside him.

"Hello, Cason, Rose." Etta called, "Good to see you again."

Cord remained in the saddle while Macara reached Rose out of the buggy and led her up on the Luce's porch. Macara introduced Cord as "Mr. Cord, come to help Maggie." Cord tipped his hat cordially and declined Etta's offer of lunch, allowing that he and Macara needed to get on with their trip.

After Rose was deposited inside the house with Etta, Macara stripped the buggy rigging from his horse and saddled up quickly. They struck out at a gallop.

Chapter Four

The door to the Tremayne house opened and Sam Luce stepped out onto the porch with Maggie Tremayne a step behind him. Sam's tall lanky frame all but hid Maggie from view. As he placed the big floppy brown hat on his head, Maggie's hand went to his elbow. He turned to face the small blond woman and assumed a stance that conveyed embarrassment, knowing what was coming.

Maggie smiled that big toothy smile that lit up her entire face and spoke the words that she knew she did not need to say but had to say anyway for her own peace of mind: "Sam, I know I said this before but thank you for all your help. I couldn't do it without you."

"Ain't doing it for thanks, doing it 'cause it needs doing." Sam said, automatically, tugging at his scruffy grey beard. This was the part of being here that was the hardest for him. Sam Luce was a doer, not a talker, and was always uncomfortable with this sort of thing, especially being thanked for something that he did, as he said, because it needed doing.

"You're a better man than you make yourself out to be, Sam Luce, and I'll never stop thanking you." Maggie said softly.

Sam grinned and turned to move to his mount, tethered at the porch post. With one motion, he grabbed the pommel and swung his long body neatly into the saddle. He tugged at his hat to be sure it was tightly seated and started to say his goodbye, "You take care, Maggie . . ." He stopped when he saw Maggie look away from him and out toward the knoll that opened onto her property. Sam craned his neck to see what Maggie was straining to see, what was drawing her attention. Whether it was Sam's keen eye or his perspective was not clear, but Sam was able sooner than Maggie to recognize the images coming over the knoll.

"Cason." he announced, "Stranger with him."

Maggie nodded and Sam turned his horse to face the oncoming pair. Both set about waiting for the two riders to make their way to the house.

At a loping gait, Macara and Cord directed their mounts to the Tremayne home and drew up facing Sam Luce. Sam knew by the expressions on their faces that these men were not on a social call. He nodded to both as Macara spoke.

"Morning to you, Sam. Etta said you'd be here."

"Just about to head home." Sam replied tersely. "You take care now."

With that, Sam, not one to ask questions or nose into anyone's business, pulled his horse around and struck out for the knoll and home, where he knew he was now needed.

Macara and Cord dismounted and tied off their mounts to the same post Sam had just vacated. As Macara approached Maggie, his face forced a smile of reassurance to silently answer the questioning look on her own countenance. He took her hand in a touching fatherly gesture that put her immediately at ease. "Ah, you look tired, lassie."

"I don't know what I'd do without you and Sam and the others' help. There's so much . . ." Maggie trailed off and her thoughts drifted to Will and how much he did when he was alive. He was a dynamo, she thought. I can't do it all . . .

Macara patted her hand and that brought her back to reality. She looked past him to the man who had accompanied him, this tall gentle seeming man whose look was also that of a helper. With a sideways turn, Macara gestured to Cord. "Maggie, lass, this is U.S. Marshal, Mr. Cord, here to bring this horrid situation to justice."

Cord stepped forward, removing his hat. "I'm pleased to make your acquaintance, m'am, and I'm real sorry about your husband." His voice was strong but compassionate and she felt the gentleness of his touch when she took his extended hand. "I do need to take down your statement of what happened, if you feel up to it."

The events of that night suddenly were at the forefront of her mind again and her eyes began to well up with the memory of it. She fought back the coming tears and looked Cord straight in the eye. "I'm likewise pleased to meet you, Mr. Cord. And yes, I can tell you exactly what happened." Maggie's manners took hold and she gestured toward the open door of the house. "Won't you please come in and be comfortable?"

"Thank you, m'am." Cord said simply and followed Maggie inside. Macara entered behind them and stepped off to the side to allow Cord to conduct the business at hand.

"Mrs. Tremayne," Cord began officially, "this is an official statement that will be read in court so I'm going to need to swear you in."

"I have a bible." Maggie stated, almost without thought, as she turned to the shelf on which the book rested.

"As you wish, m'am."

Maggie lifted the bible from the shelf and placed it on the table that was in the center of the room. She placed her left hand on the book and raised her right hand, ready to be sworn. Cord wondered briefly how this simple woman was aware of court procedures, but put that aside and proceeded to administer the oath. When Maggie acknowledged the oath, Cord made a suggestion: "You may want to sit down for this."

"If you will also, Marshal." Maggie offered.

Cord occupied the chair in front of him and produced pencil and paper, ready to record the statement. "Thank you. Now please tell me what happened on the night of May seventh."

Maggie began her statement in a very matter-of-fact manner, telling how Will had taken to camping in the barn part of each night to deter further thefts. She continued in that vein until the point at which her eyes met those of Oren Rudabaugh. Then she became agitated. Her face showed the anger that was seething inside her. "I saw him on the horse and I knew he'd done something to Will. Then he shot at me and I dove right into that pile of hay. I don't know how he missed me, he was so close. Then he was gone. I heard the horse run out of the barn and away, and then I heard Will calling me."

Cord interrupted Maggie, "Can you identify that man if you see him again?"

"Mr. Cord, he killed my Will. I will never forget that man's face as long as I live."

Cord nodded and allowed her to continue to the conclusion of the statement without further interruption. "And you're sure your husband said Oren Rudabaugh."

"Yes, Marshal, I'm certain."

Cord secured Maggie's signature on the document and deposited it in his shirt pocket. He regarded the woman before him, who was staring at him questioningly. He was touched by her plight and suddenly felt the need to console her, to hold her, to do what he could to make her believe that things would work out. He deferred that, however, to Macara who was now making his way to accomplish that purpose. The touch of Macara's hand on her shoulder broke her intensity and allowed her to speak.

"Will you kill him, Mr. Cord? Will you kill Oren Rudabaugh? I want him dead." She was staring him right in the eye again and this made Cord a tad uncomfortable.

"M'am, I am going to arrest Oren Rudabaugh for murder and take him back to Denver to stand trial. If he's convicted, he'll hang. But, m'am, I am not planning to kill anyone." Cord's words were harsh, perhaps, but this was his job she was talking about and he was not going to let her get the wrong idea of how he was going to do it.

Maggie buried her face in her hands and sobbed quietly as Macara stroked her shoulder. "I did not mean to upset you, m'am," Cord continued, "but I'm an officer of the law, not a killer."

Maggie reached out a hand to Cord's forearm. "I apologize, Marshal. I did not mean to imply that. It's just that I hate that man so thoroughly that I'm not thinking straight. Of course the law should prevail and you should do your duty fairly."

"I do understand how you feel," Cord stated, "but for this to be legal it has to be done the right way. I'll arrest Rudabaugh, you'll identify him, he'll be tried and he'll hang. I'm certain of that."

Maggie uttered a quiet thank you through her tears.

"Mrs. Tremayne," Cord began, partly trying to change the subject and partly continuing with the investigation, "would it be all right if I take a look around the barn?"

Maggie's manner changed abruptly. "Of course. I'll take you out there."

"If it's all the same to you, I'd prefer to look it over alone. I don't want to disturb the scene any more than has been done already."

Maggie nodded agreement as Cord rose from the table and moved to the door. Macara came around to assume Cord's position in the chair and took Maggie's hands in his.

"It'll be all right, lass, it'll be all right." Cord heard Macara remark as he stepped through the door and made his way to the area of the barn. Putting his Indian training to use, he observed the ground in front of the barn door, noting the tracks of several horses as well as varied boot prints, which he allowed were those of Macara and Sam Luce as they removed the body from the barn. Sketchy buggy tracks were also available, those of Macara's buggy, no doubt. Also quite prevalent were Maggie's unmistakable footprints, marking her many trips between the house and the barn. With the intention of disturbing as little as possible, Cord opened the barn door wide, but kept against the door jamb as he entered the barn and stood there surveying the scene. From the daylight that the big door allowed in, he observed a different set of boot prints. Big they were, bigger than any others there. And the tracks of the horse were miraculously still visible, even after the amount of time passed. He noted the shoe print of one hoof, displaying a support brace on the back of the shoe, a procedure sometimes used to tend a sore hoof. He made quick work of the rest of the scene, noting the hay pile into which Maggie dove to avoid the assailant's bullet and the stall next to it where Will Tremayne breathed his last. Blood was still present on the wall of the stall.

As Cord exited the barn, he turned to his right to follow the hoof prints which marked the assailant's escape. He could see the gallop stride as the horse made off. And, ever present, was the print of the shoe with the support brace. Cord, deep in observance, began to feel that he was being watched and turned to see Macara and Maggie standing on the house porch. He strode quickly toward them, speaking as he walked.

"Did the horse have a problem with one hoof?"

"Yes," Maggie answered quickly, "she split her hoof and Will put a brace on the shoe to help it mend. Why?"

"I'll be able to track that horse with no problems to wherever she is now. That should make finding Rudabaugh much easier."

"I can make it easier still." Macara offered. "I can take you right to the Rudabaugh camp. I've been out there a couple of times to mend their wounds."

"I thank you for the offer but I can't let you do that." Cord stated. "I'd be putting to you in danger. I'd best play this out alone."

Macara appeared to be prepared for this and already had an argument planned. "Sure, there can be no danger in taking you to them. You don't know the country, you don't know where their sentry is posted. You'd be a sitting duck. It's an armed camp up there, lad. No one goes in or out without permission."

"I have no intention of just riding into the camp plain as day. I've had plenty of practice at this. Besides, I can't put a civilian into danger just to make it easier. It doesn't work that way." Cord was trying to be reasonable as well as forceful to get his point across.

"Then deputize me. So help me, lad, I'm your best hope at this."

"I appreciate your wanting to help but . . ."

"Look, it's not wanting to help, it's needing to help. These are my people here. They look to me to protect them. I've done a pretty poor job of it to now, but that's going to change. I should have sent for you when this thing started instead of waiting. Will might still be with us if I had. But I'll now do what I need to do, with or without permission."

Cord observed the resolve in Macara's statement and decided to end the argument. "You're deputized."

Macara stopped in his tracks, fully expecting to continue the exchange. "What?"

Cord smiled. "I said you're deputized. I'd rather have you riding with me than trailing behind me, which I'm certain you would do."

"That's true."

"But, if you ride with me, it's my rules and my decisions."

"Understood."

Maggie took a step to Macara and touched his arm. "Cason, you take care now." Then turning to Cord, she continued, "Both of you take care."

Cord nodded and touched the brim of his hat respectfully. Macara smiled and patted Maggie's hand. But her gaze stayed with Cord as he started toward his horse. There was a strange inexplicable connection that she was experiencing between herself and the lawman. As quickly as it manifested itself was as quickly as she dispatched it.

"Come on, deputy," Cord called. "Let's get started."

Chapter Five

The better part of the afternoon was consumed by Macara and Cord in the saddle. As they exited a canyon, Cord called a halt. He removed his hat and produced a kerchief to mop the sweatband.

"How much farther?" he asked.

"At this pace, about another hour." was Macara's reply.

"That's going to put us close to dark." Cord observed. "Can you find your way into the camp after dark?"

"Aye. But we'll still need to get past the sentry, night· or day."

"How does the sentry work? Does he stop you or just start shooting?"

"He'll stop you and take you to Asa Rudabaugh. He's the clan leader, and a woeful soul he is too. Nothing gets done without his say-so."

"And there's only one sentry?"

"Aye. With the vantage point he has, there's only need for one."

Cord thought a moment then spoke. "All right then. We'll go in at night and let the sentry spot us. Between the two of us, I believe we can get the drop on him. Once he's out of the way, we can get into the camp and arrest Oren Rudabaugh."

"It'll not be that easy. Asa's got a lot of firepower up there."

Cord thought another moment. "I've got some ideas about that. We'll see as we go what needs to be done. Right now, let's find a place to camp until dark."

Macara pointed off to the right. "There's a stream the other side of the tree line. Good camping there."

The two riders directed their mounts toward the tree line.

Camping along the stream afforded the pair plenty of fresh water to brew coffee. They drew closer to the small fire as darkness descended and a chill filled the air. They donned jackets to ward off the cooler air. Some dried beef replenished their energy and the coffee fought the sleepiness that the approaching darkness was promoting.

After eating, Macara succumbed to the desire for a smoke. He produced a pipe from his shirt pocket and rose to fetch his tobacco pouch from his britches. As the pouch came out, a small shiny object exited with it and fell to the ground. It caught Cord's attention and he announced: "You dropped something."

Macara looked down and retrieved the object. He fingered it gently and a whimsical look came over his face. "Saint Christopher." he said by way of introduction to the medal. "Given to me by me first love back in the old country."

Cord looked up in interest as Macara returned to a sitting position.

"You know, I still miss her and it's been all these years. A fair lass she was and more than a seventeen year old lad that I was could handle. And married she was.

She's the reason I'm here today and not back in Ireland. When her husband found out about us, I had to go or he would have killed me sure. She gave me this to see me safely through me journeys. Little did she know that I'd be traveling so far."

"Never been back?" Cord asked.

"Never." Macara continued, "Once I signed on that ship in London Harbor, I was already a world away. I wanted to come to America but it took three years to get to Boston. By then I'd had it with life on the sea, a hard life it is, little food and rest and endless work. But Saint Christopher did his work and got me there safe." He fingered the medal as he spoke.

"It's a long way from Boston to here." Cord observed.

"Aye, but by then I'd had the wanderlust. Boston was too big and populated so I pushed west. Got myself hurt in the Dakotas and was nursed back to health by an Indian maid, Rose's mother. That was a selfless woman now. Gave her all to our relationship and perished in childbirth. I scooped up me Rose and went on." Macara stopped just long enough to strike a match and puff the pipe to life. "Finally stopped here to find some peace and raise her proper." Macara's attention span shifted. "But enough about me. You seem well schooled and able. What caused you to take such a dangerous position as a United States Marshal?"

The question caught Cord unaware. He was ordinarily a man of few words, and almost always not about himself. But the openness that Macara's conversation had created sucked him in and he readily answered. "My father was a police detective in Washington, D.C. I grew up with the law as a way of life. It just seemed a natural fit. Like you, I did not take to city life so after the war and my time with the Apache, I became a marshal. Been there ever since."

Cord was amazed that he had said this much. It seemed that Macara's easy going way and honesty about himself was contagious.

"You spent time with the Apaches?" Macara was more curious now.

"Yes," Cord continued, "almost a year. After the war, I transferred to the Indian Territory. Got interested in their way of life and, after I was mustered out, I lived with them awhile. Learned a lot that I still use today. They are why I can track so well and survive out here."

"That's the first good words I've heard about the Apache." There was surprise in Macara's voice.

"They're just trying to survive like the rest of us."

"Aye. I suppose so."

As quickly as it started, the conversation ended there. When it was dark enough, Cord rose and dumped the balance of the coffee on the fire.

"Time to go." he said quietly.

Macara got to his feet bearing a new regard for this tall complex man with whom he was riding. There was much more to this lad than met the eye.

They saddled up and mounted and struck out once more for the Rudabaugh camp. Macara would use every bit of the memory of his previous trips to the camp to navigate the journey in the dark.

They finished the trip in just under an hour. As they drew rein at the beginning of a large clearing, well within the cover of trees, Macara leaned in close so his voice would not carry.

"The guard sits on a knoll just off to the left of the far side of the clearing. He's got a full view of every movement in the clearing. He'll let you get about three quarters of the way to the brush on the far side, then he'll stop you. You've no place to run. You're right out in the open. He'll ride out to meet you and have you dismount, and he'll search you. Then you go into the camp. You walk and lead your horse. The guard rides behind you. You'll not be out of his sight for an instant."

"So his attention is constantly on you, right?"

"Aye."

"That's good. He'll not pay much attention to what's going on around him after he stops you."

"Aye."

"That's exactly what I need."

Macara flashed a quizzical look at Cord. "What have you got in mind, lad?"

Cord gazed off into the clearing for a few seconds, as if to visualize what his mind was constructing. Then he reached out the Winchester rifle from its saddle scabbard and handed it out to Macara. "Ever seen one of these before?" he asked.

Macara studied the weapon carefully and concluded that he had not seen its like. "No." he stated tentatively, now burning with curiosity. What did Cord have up his sleeve?

"This is a Winchester 1873 model repeater. Not too many of these up here in these parts. Are you certain that guard will not shoot anyone out of the saddle on sight?"

"Aye." was Macara's anxious answer as he also nodded.

Cord leaned even closer. "If you're willing, here's what I've got planned: you will ride across the clearing as if you're making a call on the camp and let the guard capture you. You will have this rifle in plain sight. Besides the guard's attention on you, I want his attention on the rifle. It'll be quite a find to him. I want him totally engrossed in you and the gun so I can move in from behind and take him. I don't want a shot fired to alarm the camp. We'll do this Indian style, quick and quiet. Can you do this?"

Macara hesitated for a second, studied the weapon and looked back at Cord. "You're going to kill him quick and quiet?"

Cord took in a breath and a look of dissatisfaction came over his face. Why do people keep thinking I'm a killer, he quizzed himself. "I'm not going to kill anyone. I'm going to take him down, tie him up and place him where he can't cause any trouble. Now, are you with me on this?"

Macara breathed a sigh of relief. The thought of possibly being part of a killing gave him pause. But to take a captive without harm, this he could do. "I am." he stated and took possession of the weapon.

"Good. Now then, give me about ten minutes to get through this brush over here and get to a spot where I can move in from behind. When you start out, don't be quiet about it. Ride in like you're expected, and let that Winchester be seen. Do exactly as the guard says. I'll take care of the rest."

Macara watched as Cord directed his horse into the thick brush on the left side of the clearing and disappeared into the night. Aside from the initial rustling of hooves as Cord entered the brush, Macara heard nothing more than the crickets. He began counting the seconds to give Cord the delay he required.

At the end of what he was sure was ten minutes, Macara goosed his mount with his heels and entered the clearing. He cradled the Winchester across his saddle just behind the pommel and rode confidently, all the while trying to control his heart from beating right out of his chest. He was here to make a call. He had been sent for to take care of an injured man and this was his mission. This was his story when he would be stopped by the guard. This, and prominently displaying the rifle he carried would keep the guard busy until Cord came. He prayed God that it would come out that way. But, yet he trusted Cord to know what he was doing and to be able to pull this off. He was now about half way across the clearing and it seemed like an eternity since he had started. His eyes scanned the area of the knoll where the guard would be waiting, hoping to catch an early sign of the man, but to no avail. Cautiously, but with that confident appearance, Macara kept riding.

On the knoll slightly above the clearing, Grey Tumbley sat comfortably on a rock with his Henry rifle in the crook of his arm. He was an average size man with a bit of a paunch that was more evident from a sitting position. His belly hung a bit over his belt and bulged somewhat against his dirty salmon colored shirt. His yellow hair shot uncontrollably out from under his battered brown hat and his face was covered with a scruffy yellow growth of beard. As he scanned the clearing, he became aware of movement on the other side. He strained to make out the figure down there and was satisfied that it was a lone rider. There was nothing particularly suspicious about the rider. As a matter of fact, he felt that he had seen the person before. He sat up a bit straighter and set about waiting for the visitor to arrive at what he called the challenge spot, the spot where he would stop the rider and check him out.

As the rider reached the spot, Tumbley rose and sighted in with his rifle. "Hold up there, mister. You covered." he said in a thick southern accented gravelly voice.

Macara immediately reined in and watched as Tumbley appeared from behind some bushes, rifle sighted on him. A sitting duck I am, he told himself, as if it was not old news.

"Keep your hands where I can see them and step down off'n that horse." Tumbley continued as he cautiously approached. Macara complied and kept his hands in the air with the rifle raised above his head.

Tumbley reached Macara in a few seconds and lowered his rifle to a position adjacent to his hip, just above his sidearm. "Drop that rifle in front of you and step back two paces." Tumbley ordered.

Macara again obediently complied.

"State your business here." was Tumbley's next command.

"Me name is Cason Macara." Macara began. "Asa Rudabaugh sent for me to tend to an injured man. I came as soon as I could, you know. How bad is the injury?" He hoped his attempt to engage the man in conversation would occupy his attention.

"Don't know what you're talking about, friend. Don't know of no injured man. We'll see what Asa has to say about this. Get hold of your reins and start moving."

"What about me rifle?" Macara asked, trying for more delay. "Wouldn't want to lose that one. It's a good one." He felt that his efforts were getting weaker. Where the hell was Cord anyway?

"Hold your ground." Tumbley ordered. He then squatted while covering Macara and reached up the Winchester from the dirt. The weapon immediately caught his eye, even in the dark, the bright moonlight glinting off the weapon's surface. This was one of them Winchester repeaters he had heard about. This would sit well on his saddle, he thought, as he continued to peruse the weapon.

The poke in his back brought him immediately back to reality, as did the words softly spoken into his ear: "Move and you're a dead man!" Tumbley instinctively froze. Whether that object in his back was a knife or a gun did not matter. He knew he was buffaloed and so he obeyed. The figure behind him kept the pressure on his back as he pulled first one rifle, then the other from his hands. The weapons clattered on the ground a safe distance away.

Macara breathed a heavy sigh of relief and smiled as he watched Cord manipulate the guard. The Indians' lessons were well taught. Cord had never made a sound on his approach.

"Hands behind your head." was Cord's next command. Tumbley obeyed smartly. Cord returned the knife to its sheath on his gun belt and drew his sidearm in its place. "Turn around. Mind you, do it slow." Tumbley complied. When he faced his adversary, even in the dark, recognition registered immediately. "Cord?" It was both a question and a statement.

It took Cord a second or two to pull the man's identity from his memory but then: "Hello, Grey, fancy meeting you here! How long have you been out? Doesn't seem like five years."

"Four and a half. Got six months off for good behavior." Tumbley seemed proud of that fact.

"And what might you be doing here?"

"Working for Asa Rudabaugh. He hired me a while back."

"Hired your gun is more to the point."

"I ain't broke no laws, Cord, not since I'm out now. This is honest work."

"We'll see about that." Cord stated, breaking off the conversation and returning to the business at hand. "Now then, I'm putting you out of commission for a time."

With a shrug, Cord caused the coil of rope on his shoulder to slip down his arm to his hand where it was caught. Cord secured Tumbley's hands behind his back with the rope, cutting off the end with his knife, and then produced the kerchief from his back pocket to use as a gag. Once Tumbley's horse was located, Cord directed Tumbley into the brush at the base of the knoll and secured the man's tied hands to a stout bush with more rope. Then the man's feet were tied together and the horse was tethered nearby.

As he turned to leave the secured man, Cord told him: "I'd advise you to stay put till someone finds you. You don't want to get mixed up in what's about to happen next."

Chapter Six

The Rudabaugh camp was a collection of wooden lean-tos, tents and the like in a clearing about a mile and a half from the guard's location. Surrounded by huge slabs of mountain rock, the clearing boasted only one entrance from the thick brush that separated it from the guard's location. Off to the left of the entrance, a makeshift corral contained half a dozen or so horses. To the right was a dugout, a living area excavated into the earth and supplied with steps and a door fashioned from split logs tied together with stout rope. The door was only half visible from the ground's surface. The entire camp was quiet save for the baleful wale of a harmonica that drifted out from one of the tents. The evening meal had been consumed and now the camp's occupants were drinking themselves to sleep, except for the incessant harmonica player.

The door to the dugout opened abruptly and Asa Rudabaugh stepped his hulking frame through the opening. Clad in a red union suit shirt and rudimentary buckskin pants, his body seemed to bulge out of the clothing. His ruddy round face was almost completely covered in beard and overgrown hair. In his hand he carried a jug that could not be mistaken for anything but liquor.

It was the harmonica that elicited his appearance in the doorway. "Quit that goddam caterwauling." the great booming voice commanded. The music stopped almost immediately. Rudabaugh took a long pull on the jug and turned back inside the dugout.

"We'll be checking the trap line in the morning." Rudabaugh said, apparently continuing the conversation that was interrupted by his distaste for the harmonica music, "Then we got to get the still going again. We're low on this stuff." He hoisted the jug to indicate the object of his statement.

Oren Rudabaugh looked up from his seat on the bunk and nodded. He was as big as Asa but without the middle-aged paunchiness. His solid frame seemed too large to be occupying the dugout with his uncle, but apparently both fitted as comfortably as possible in the area. He was a much younger man, just out of his teens and all muscle. Oren wore the same cut of clothing as his uncle, but his sandy hair and beard were shorter than the older Rudabaugh.

"Before we go, I want to check my horse's hoof." Oren said in a voice an octave higher than his uncle. "The brace that sodbuster put on it seems like it worked but I want to be sure."

"Don't need no mount pulling up lame while we're out." Asa agreed. He sat on his own bunk across the tiny room and continued drinking.

Cord and Macara approached the camp on foot, leading their horses. As the clearing came into sight, Cord placed a hand over his horse's nose to stifle any noise the animal might make upon recognition of the horses in the camp's corral. Macara saw the merit in the move and did the same to his own mount. Under the cover of thick brush, they surveyed the scene and spoke in whispers.

"The dugout is where Rudabaugh and his nephew stay." Macara informed Cord. "Only one way in or out."

"Once we get in, we'll get out." Cord stated. "But we need a way in."

Cord leaned out further to get a better picture of the layout. As he looked, he formulated a plan to gain entrance into the dugout. He turned back to Macara. "We're going to get some assistance from one of the men outside the dugout. Follow me and don't make a sound. We need to find just one man so we don't disturb the others."

Macara nodded and followed Cord as he made his way along the edge of the brush to different vantage points. His search for a one occupant enclosure led them to the man with the harmonica. Cord placed them on either side of the open tent flap and Cord carefully peered inside. The dim lantern light revealed the man's back turned to the opening. He was on his knees hovering over the parts of his disassembled rifle. In two long steps, Cord was upon the man and his knife went to the man's throat. His other hand went over the man's mouth to quiet a possible alarm. Cord spoke in a harsh whisper: "Don't move. Don't even twitch." The man went slightly limp to indicate acquiescence.

Macara slipped inside the tent and waited just inside the opening.

Cord took his hand from the man's mouth and the knife from his throat. But the knife was immediately placed at the man's back to indicate that he was still covered.

"I'm a U.S. Marshal." Cord said. "I'm looking for Oren Rudabaugh and you're going to take us to him. Right?" The last word was emphasized with more pressure of the knife on the man's back. The man nodded quickly.

"Now then, very quickly and very quietly, take us to him."

The man rose to his feet and led the pair silently across the area, avoiding the other residences so as not to raise an alarm. As they passed the corral, one of the horses whinnied. The trio stopped cold for a second until Cord was satisfied that no one reacted to the noise. They then continued to the dugout and descended the stone steps.

Cord leaned to the man's ear and whispered, "Get them to open this door."

The man raised his hand and knocked tentatively on the log door. A second later, the door moved slightly inward. With a great shove against the man's body, Cord forced his way forward, throwing the door wide open. The man plummeted into Asa's body, who, off balance and slightly drunk, fell backward. The two men landed in a heap on the dirt floor of the dugout.

Startled by the activity, Oren sprang from his lying position on the bunk to come face to face with Cord, who, by now, was inside the doorway and leveling his revolver on the group. Macara quickly entered and closed the door to keep any noise from escaping and alerting the camp. Asa shoved the harmonica man away from him and rolled to his feet, stunned slightly by the activity. As

Oren made a move toward his gun on the bunk, Cord's terse command, "Hold it!" stopped each man cold.

Asa regained some composure and with it came anger. "What the hell is going on here?" he demanded, "What do you want?"

Cord reached to the bunk and fetched Oren's Colt. "I'll ask the questions. Which one of you is Oren Rudabaugh?"

"That's me." was Oren's tentative answer.

"You're under arrest for the murder of Will Tremayne." Cord said as he jammed Oren's weapon into his waistband.

Oren's jaw dropped and, as he was about to speak, Asa chimed in, "Who the hell do you think you are, coming in here, bold as you please."

"Name's Cord. I'm a U.S. Marshal. He's coming with me."

"Ain't likely." Asa retorted. "Nobody's taking my kin nowhere. You'll have to walk over me and my boys before that happens. I'm calling them in here right now."

"And you'll be the first to go down." Cord stated. "Now he's going out of here with me. Get that through your head. If you get in my way, you'll go with him, one way or another. That goes for anyone else that interferes."

Asa went silent, understanding that Cord meant business and seemed willing to do whatever was necessary to make this happen.

Oren turned to his uncle. "Uncle Asa, you can't let him take me." he pleaded.

Asa never took his eyes off Cord, but counseled his nephew: "Don't you fret none, Oren. This ain't over yet."

Cord moved to the near wall of the dugout and grabbed some rawhide thongs hanging on a spike. Moving to the harmonica man, who was still in a heap where Asa had shoved him, Cord dropped the thongs next to him and ordered him to bind Oren's hands.

When it was done, Cord moved behind the group and issued his next command: "Now then, outside. And don't get any notions."

Macara opened the door and the group moved outside as ordered, with Cord and Macara bringing up the rear. When they were well into the clearing, Cord raised his revolver in the air and discharged one shot. It split the quiet night loudly and, seconds later, elicited the reaction Cord desired. With a flurry of feet and weapons, the occupants of the camp turned out of their quarters in a confused but ready state. As their eyes adjusted to the moonlight, Cord's voice stopped them where they were. "I'm a United States Marshal. I'm here to arrest Oren Rudabaugh. Drop your weapons and stand down."

"Get him, boys." Asa boomed. The disjointed group began to advance. Cord's gun immediately went to within an inch of Asa's head. "I meant what I said, you idiot." Cord cocked the pistol loudly. "Now call them off."

Asa considered for a second and thought better of the action. His opportunity would come at another time. "Wait. Back off." he called. The group stopped as one.

"Toss the guns away, as far as you can." Cord commanded. Pistols and rifles landed a safe distance away as the group complied. Cord lowered the hammer on the revolver and directed the entire group to the corral. "Is the Tremayne horse here?" he asked Macara.

Macara looked over the remuda and picked out the Tremayne horse. "That bay there." he answered, pointing.

Cord grabbed the arm of the harmonica man. "Saddle that bay and tie her to the corral." He then turned to Macara. "Cason, will you get our horses please?"

"Aye." Macara said as he started out for the brush.

The harmonica man quickly saddled the bay and tied her off to a corral post as instructed. By that time, Macara was returning with their mounts. Cord's next order had the harmonica man open the corral gate once again. His first shot had stirred the animals and made them skittish. Another two shots now drove the horses through the open corral gate and into the night as far away from the disturbing noise as they could get.

Asa pondered Cord's actions and concluded that he was dealing with a worthy adversary, one who seemed to have all the plans in place to pull this off. But this was not over. Not hardly.

Cord ordered Oren into the saddle of the bay horse, and then he and Macara mounted. Cord's last statement was directed to Asa: "If anyone tries anything, my prisoner is a dead man." and the trio started off to leave the camp. Once they were out of sight, Asa cried out: "Go find them horses." He stooped down and grabbed a rock from the ground and angrily flung it in the general direction that Cord and his party had taken. As the group scurried off to locate and retrieve the horses, Asa took two steps forward and called: "This ain't hardly over, lawman. You hear me? This ain't over."

Chapter Seven

Ten minutes at full gallop put enough distance between the fleeing trio and the Rudabaugh camp for Cord to call a halt to rest the horses. "Light and take a breather." he told Macara. As Macara stepped down from the saddle, Cord led the Tremayne horse with Oren Rudabaugh aboard to a stout branch and tied off the reins. Cord dismounted and ordered Oren out of the saddle. The young man complied. "Sit." was Cord's next order. Oren folded his legs under himself and crouched. "I said sit." Cord corrected, "Legs straight out in front of you." Oren grumbled and executed the order. Cord was taking no chances with this prisoner and placing him in a position from which it would be difficult to recover was insurance that he could keep the upper hand while he rested.

Macara stepped to Cord and placed a hand on his shoulder. "I've got to hand it to you, lad. I had me doubts that we could pull this off."

"We're not out of the woods yet. Asa's not going to sit back and let this happen without a fight. Our best bet is to get to familiar ground and get Oren locked up. Then we can deal with Asa straight on."

"Then we'll head for my place. We can lock him away and have plenty of cover."

"Cason," Cord took a counseling tone, "I know this is closing the barn door after the horse is gone, but are you sure you've considered what's involved here? You have to live here. I'm taking him back to Denver for trial and my job's done, but you'll be here among these animals. They can play pretty rough."

"I've done me thinking, lad, and I'm seeing this through." Macara resolved, "I've moved on for the last time. This is my home now and that of the people around me and I'll give no quarter to those that'd take it from us."

"What about your daughter?"

"Now, a fine father I'd be if I couldn't stand up for our rights. My Rose will grow up in a law abiding community, I promise you that."

Oren's drawl interrupted the conversation: "There won't be nothing left of any of you when my uncle gets done with you."

Cord's glare at Oren was intense. "Never mind making threats, mister. You've got just one thing to ponder on. You're going to Denver to stand trial and Mrs. Tremayne's testimony will hang you. Anyone that tries to interfere with that will go down with you. Now then, on your feet. We're moving out."

Grey Tumbley worked diligently on the ropes that bound his hands and finally was able to dislodge the knots. He furiously tugged at the ropes until his hands were free, then untied his legs and got to his feet. His legs were shaky from being tied but he managed to make his way to his horse. He checked his holster to find that his sidearm was still there. Then he remembered his rifle and stumbled to the area where Cord had tossed it. Having secured the weapon, he swung his frame into the saddle and struck out for the Rudabaugh camp. At full gallop, the ride took only moments but it afforded Tumbley time to further work up his anger for Cord. It was not enough that Cord had tracked him down and sent him to prison. Now he appeared out of nowhere to again interfere with his life. This time Cord will pay, he swore. "I'll see him crawl in front of my gun before I kill him." was his pledge.

The horse broke into the clearing at the Rudabaugh camp on a dead run and Tumbley hauled on the reins to halt the animal as he swung down from the saddle. A quick glance around the moonlit area told him that it was empty, not even a horse in the corral. "Asa." he called as he trotted toward the dugout.

At the same time, the dugout door opened and Asa strode up the steps to ground level to face Tumbley. "Where the hell have you been?" he demanded.

Tumbley fell back a step, reacting to Asa's wrath. "They jumped me." he offered in excuse. "Two of them."

Asa took a step forward and swatted the man with the back of his hand. The blow caught Tumbley's jaw and opened a trickle of blood at the corner of his mouth as he reeled back and faltered to the ground. He raised both hands outstretched as if to ward off any further strikes.

"They took Oren. You was supposed to stop them before they got in here. Now they got Oren and the horses are scattered and we can't get after them till the boys get the horses back."

"I'm sorry, Asa." Tumbley cringed. "But I got my horse. I can get after them right now. I got a score to settle with them two anyway. I'll get Oren back for you."

"All right, get going. We'll follow as soon as we can."

Tumbley scrambled to his feet and hauled himself into the saddle. With a great tug on the reins, he pulled the horse around and broke into full gallop as he left the camp. As soon as he was clear of the camp he slowed the mount down and tried to track Cord and his party in the moonlight. His tracking skills left much to be desired, but he was able to spot the brace on the shoe of the horse Oren had stolen. He assumed that Oren was on that horse and so he would follow those tracks.

Following his assumption bore fruit once more distance had been put between himself and the camp. The tracks were clearer and told him that he was following three horsemen. He followed the tracks all night and into the early hours of the morning. As first light broke, Tumbley found himself at the crest of a ridge which afforded him a panoramic view of the country before him. Thankfully, the light was brightening and, by straining his eyesight he was able to make out three riders progressing forward several miles ahead.

A quick survey of the area allowed him to formulate a plan. By riding the crest of this ridge at full gallop, he estimated that he could overtake the trio and lay a trap for them ahead. Without further pause, he urged his mount to a gallop and continued along the ridge. It was a treacherous journey through heavy brush but he would not let the horse slow. There was too much at stake. He needed to rectify his standing with Asa, he needed to free

Oren, and he needed to kill Cord. He resolved that he would accomplish all three tasks in one.

As he progressed, Tumbley was able to periodically spot the riders and gather that he was in fact overtaking them. He pressed on until the ridge descended to the level of the ground on which the trio was riding. At that point, he stopped in a thick barrage of trees and selected suitable cover that afforded him a clear view of the trail in front of him. He tied off his mount and fetched the Henry from the saddle holster. There would not be much time before the riders appeared and he wanted to be sure he could be comfortable enough in his cover so his shots would count. Cord would be his first target and he swore he would hit him with the first shot.

Chapter Eight

As the trio approached the tall boulder which marked a sharp turn in the trail, Cord became instinctively apprehensive and slowed the gait from a trot to a walk. If his instincts were correct and danger lurked around this bend, he wanted to be traveling slowly enough to react before they were completely in the open. He signaled to Macara to proceed with care and Macara nodded.

The trail broke sharply to the left, placing Cord in the position of first around the turn. His eyes scanned the scene before him carefully, hoping to spot any trouble beforehand. He could see nothing. The party advanced in single file with Cord in the lead and Macara bringing up the rear, sandwiching Oren in the middle. Oren's hands were now tied in front of him instead of behind him so he could control his horse.

Tumbley had Cord in his sights now and was leading him with the point of the rifle. His finger slowly tightened on the trigger as he waited for just the right moment to strike. He was in a crouch position behind a fallen tree with his boot heel dug into the ground for support. His body tensed as he prepared to fire. A twitch in his leg caused the boot to slip slightly and the shot snapped off a second too soon.

Cord felt the bullet scoop the hat off his head and a split second later heard the report of the Henry. His horse jerked slightly. His mind went to work immediately, locating the origin of the shot by the puff of black smoke in the tree line and, at the same time, waiving Macara toward an outcropping of rocks to gain cover. His revolver came up quickly and fired two wild shots in the general direction of the smoke to keep the assailant's head down while they made for cover.

Macara came around the outside of Oren intending to also direct him toward the outcropping of rocks, but Oren was already urging his mount forward in a hasty escape attempt. A second shot from the tree line, although it did not find its mark, convinced Macara to join Cord in the run for cover. Reaching the rocks quickly, they dismounted and Cord emptied his pistol in the direction of the fleeing Oren. More shots came from the tree line, ricocheting off the rocks in front of Cord and Macara, causing them to duck below the rocks.

Now Oren was into the trees searching for what he knew was one of the boys trying to rescue him. He followed the shots from the Henry and the resultant smoke and came upon Tumbley. He dismounted and joined the man.

"You okay?" Tumbley asked.

"Yeah," Oren answered, "Get me loose." He held up his bound hands.

Tumbley produced a small knife from his pocket and cut the man's bonds.

"Give me your Colt." Oren demanded.

Without protest, Tumbley complied, fully expecting Oren to join him in exterminating his quarry. Instead, Oren remounted.

"Where you going?"

"Got to get rid of a witness. You hold them here. Asa will find you."

Oren wheeled the horse around and struck out through the trees, leaving a cursing Tumbley to fend for himself in the ensuing firefight.

Cord hastily reloaded and took advantage of the lull in the shooting to fetch his Winchester from its saddle holster. For the first time since he had met him, Cord realized that Macara did not have a weapon. Cord thrust the rifle at Macara and asked, "How good a shot are you?"

"I'm an excellent shot, I am." Macara crooned as he took the weapon in hand.

"Good. I make one shooter in there. I'm going to try to flank him. I need you to keep his head down."

Macara levered a round into the chamber of the Winchester and took up a firing position. "Do what you've got to do, lad. I'll keep him down." With that, he squeezed off his first shot.

In an instant, Cord disappeared into the brush that led to the tree line in which Tumbley was engulfed.

Macara's first round glanced off a tree not six feet from Tumbley's position. Tumbley took note that his objective was now equipped with rifle fire and the shooter had a good eye. He placed another shot that slammed into the rock in front of Macara. Macara returned fire, zeroing in closer to his target.

Tumbley was agitated. He had counted on his first shot taking Cord out of the fray and had hoped that Oren could help him take care of Cord's companion. Now none of this had come to pass and he was left in a two to one shootout that could go badly for him. His first instinct was to flee but that burning desire to see Cord under his gun won out and Tumbley decided to dig in and see this through. He continued to exchange shots with Macara, all the while noting that Macara's rounds were getting closer each time.

As Tumbley's Henry was approaching empty, he decided to move to a different position to acquire better sighting of his target. He pulled his leg from its support position and rolled to a sitting position.

"Hold it, Grey." Cord's words froze Tumbley. He heard Cord move behind him and decided that he was not going to get another chance to nail him. He twisted his body and brought the rifle around to sight in on Cord. He was actually aiming by sound rather than sight and pulled off a shot in the general direction of Cord's voice. Cord had stepped slightly to the left and the shot went wild. Cord's bullet hit its mark, burying itself deeply into Tumbley's left shoulder. The impact jerked Tumbley around and laid him back in the position from which he had been firing. He screamed in pain as the bullet ripped into the meaty part of his shoulder, narrowly missing the bone. Blood stained his shirt and the ground beneath him.

Cord moved in quickly and pulled the rifle from Tumbley's hand. He caught sight of the man's empty holster as he pitched the Henry out of reach and asked, "Where's your pistol?"

Tumbley was busy writhing in pain and did not answer.

"Hey," Cord called, "Where's your pistol?"

"Oren took it. Said he had to get rid of a witness." Tumbley was practically crying from the pain at this point.

The answer sent Cord's mind racing. His body ran cold. He had said too much back at the first rest stop. He had told Oren that Mrs. Tremayne's testimony would hang him and now Oren was on his way to keep her from testifying. The simple minded fool thinks he'll get away with it if she's not around to identify him. Suddenly, time was of the essence. He had to run Oren down before he got to her.

"Cason," Cord called through hands cupped over his mouth, "I've got him. Come up here quick."

"Aye." Macara called back. Immediately he was in a trot making his way to the scene.

Cord rolled Tumbley on his back through the man's painful screaming.

Macara reached them shortly and observed the wound in Tumbley's shoulder.

"Oren's on his way to kill Mrs. Tremayne." Cord stated. "I've got to get after him. Can you handle this?"

"I've seen worse, lad. Go. Go."

Macara extended the hand that carried the Winchester toward Cord and Cord quickly took the weapon.

"Try to get him back to your place. I'll meet you there directly." Cord said as he stepped around Tumbley and set out at a dead run for his mount. Macara went to one knee beside Tumbley and tore away the blood soaked shirt from the wound. "Now let's see just how bad this is." he mumbled. As he went to work on the wound, Macara heard rather than saw Cord's horse gallop from the area. He prayed God that Cord would be in time.

Chapter Nine

Oren Rudabaugh nearly wore the bay mare out pushing her to the limit of her endurance to make the Tremayne place as quickly as possible. The faster he got rid of that woman the better. Nobody was going to hang him, least of all no widow woman. With her gone, nobody can prove nothing, he thought. The horse was fast becoming winded and was slowing down. Oren realized that if the mare could not complete the trip his mission would be lost. He pulled rein and got down out of the saddle to reluctantly allow the horse to rest and recover. After a few seconds to recover himself, he checked the hoof which carried the braced shoe to be sure that there was not an issue of the horse going lame. Satisfied that this was not the case, he allowed the mare to rest and regain wind for a few minutes. Precious time as he saw it, time that was counting against his completing his extrication from this situation. Damn woman! Should have killed her too when I had the chance. Not letting this chance go by. Got to get to her. He paced back and forth while the animal regained composure. When he was certain that the horse could continue he swung back into the saddle and urged the mare back to an immediate gallop.

Cord's buckskin was a valiant animal capable of long distance running without rest. While he hated to put the horse through this, he had no choice but to solicit every ounce of strength the horse had to narrow the distance between himself and Oren. His rare stops were only to verify that his direction was true by the fact that the braced shoe prints of the bay mare were still visible. He knew where Oren was headed and hoped that the bay mare would not be as swift as his own mount. He wished that he knew of a shortcut to the Tremayne place. But as foolish as that sounded, it caused him to rein in and give it some thought. As he pondered, he visualized the lay of the land between him and the Tremayne spread. He had taken note during the trip to the Rudabaugh camp of how this area looked and remembered taking a long bend just before reaching the spot at which he was now situated. If he struck out now to the right he may be able to establish a shorter distance between himself and his destination. But should he take the chance? If he was wrong, or if he ran into rougher country that might slow him down, he could be too late. Overtaking Oren by continuing in this direction was becoming less likely. All Oren needed was a moment to kill Mrs. Tremayne. He had to reach her before Oren to ensure her safety. In a split second his decision was made. He pulled the buckskin to the right and headed up a slope at full gallop.

Oren's journey was going badly. The bay mare was not holding up well at all. This horse was not built for long distances at full speed. She was putting out everything she had but was beginning to fail. Another rest stop was necessary. Oren drew up and got down to allow the horse to breath. Next horse I steal will be a better one, he vowed. He paced again as the horse regained herself. Then he was back up on her and urging her forward.

Cord encountered harsher country during his diversion but his horse was up to the task. This was a sure-footed and confident animal, never missing a step or shying at an obstacle. Cord was even more certain now that he had made the right decision. The ground he was covering now was making more of a difference in getting him closer to Maggie Tremayne. He was not a religious man but he prayed now that he would be in time to protect Mrs. Tremayne from Oren, especially for the fact that he blamed himself for putting her in this danger. This caused him to urge the buckskin to even greater speed.

Maggie opened the cabin door and stepped back to the table to lift a basket of laundry she had just finished scrubbing. It was heavy and she struggled with it but managed to carry it to the clothes line that was strung from the back corner of the house to a nearby tree. She set the basket down and began removing clothes from it and draping them over the line. From the bottom of the basket she fetched a handful of clothespins which she used to secure the garments. When the last pin was placed, she retrieved the basket and started back toward the door. As she rounded the corner of the house and stepped up on the porch, movement caught her eye off to the left. She glanced in the direction of the movement and instantly recognized not only her bay mare but the buckskin clad rider atop the horse. It was Oren Rudabaugh, headed for her at a dead run.

Instinctively, Maggie tossed the basket and made for the door. There was a rifle in there and she was not going to give Rudabaugh a chance at her without putting up a fight. She cleared the door and spun around to reach above the door where the rifle was cradled. With her left hand on the weapon, her right hand levered a round into firing position. She had no thought of hiding or running from this man. Nor did she have any idea why he was there and not in Marshal Cord's custody. Her only reaction was that Will's killer was riding into range and this was her opportunity to pay him back for taking Will from her. With no concern for her own safety, she stepped back onto the porch and took dead aim at the approaching figure.

The rifle stock slammed into her shoulder as she squeezed off the shot. Whether it was that the man was not yet in range or that she had not aimed properly was unclear, but the round did not hit its mark. Rudabaugh kept coming fast. Now she could see that his pistol was in his hand and he was preparing to use it. She suddenly realized that she needed cover. Glancing over her shoulder, she determined that the house would afford next to useless cover. Quickly, she made for the barn.

Oren covered the distance to the house in about the same amount of time that it took Maggie to reach the barn. She threw open the big barn door as Oren came out of the saddle and strode angrily toward the structure. Maggie hunkered down behind the stall wall where Will had breathed his last and shouldered the rifle, ready for another shot. Oren reached the door and, without aiming, fired his pistol into the barn, more to frighten

Maggie and to dislodge her from cover than anything else. He took cover behind the opposite doorframe and waited.

Maggie knew she was in this now and had no way out but to fight back. Her determination had given way to fear and this interfered with her aim. Her next shot went through the open door area, never even coming close to Oren.

Content to wait her out, Oren crouched and allowed her to fire two more shots. One took a chunk of wood from the doorframe above his head. The other missed completely. That made four. He pegged another pistol round into the barn wildly, eliciting two more rifle shots from Maggie. She'll be empty soon, he thought, and ready for the taking. Soon came faster than he expected as he heard the rifle lever being worked and the welcome sound of the hammer falling on an empty chamber. He heard it again as Maggie began to panic and finally realized that she had no defense left.

A smirk covered Oren's face as he rose and stepped into the doorway. I got her now, he thought, just a matter of getting close enough so as not to miss. He stepped into the barn slowly, allowing his eyes to survey the scene. She could be anywhere. He moved closer to Maggie's hiding place, as fear built in her with every step he took. He listened. Her breathing was evident and was leading him to her. She pressed herself into the stall wall in an attempt to present the smallest target possible. Oren stepped around the wall and confronted her, towering over her crouched body. He grinned and pulled back the hammer of the Colt.

"Rudabaugh!" Cord's commanding voice split the silence in the barn. "Freeze!" Cord stood several steps inside the barn with his revolver leveled on Oren. Surprise gripped Oren as he realized he was at bay. His mind raced for a way out. Could he bargain for control by threatening to kill the woman? Could he turn on the lawman and take him? There was no place close enough to jump for cover. Oren stood transfixed, unable to think his way out of this.

"Uncock that pistol and drop it." Cord commanded.

Oren did not move. His mind had shut down and so had his body. He did not know what to do, so he did nothing.

"Do it!" Cord continued as he moved toward his quarry.

These words restarted Oren and his first thought was preservation. Cord had him dead to rights and nothing he could do would prevent Cord from killing him. He would live to fight another day. His thumb lowered the hammer of the Colt and he let the weapon loose to drop to the ground. Cord moved in quickly and shoved Oren to the ground where he would be less likely to cause trouble. Cord's boot heel caught the Colt and kicked it behind him, out of reach. He stepped into the stall to see a cowering Maggie in a clump on the ground up against the wall.

"Ma'm, are you all right?" Cord crouched as he asked the question, his gun still trained on Oren. Breathless, Maggie nodded but could not speak.

"I'm so sorry that I allowed this to happen." Cord stated.

Maggie began to sob, but attempted to regain composure at the same time. As she started to get to her feet, Cord reached to help her and they rose as one.

"I'm all right, Marshal. This is not your fault."

"I have my own ideas about that. Please, go in the house. I'll take care of him."

Maggie nodded and stepped uncertainly around the wall and out of the barn.

Cord thanked the Lord that he was in time to save the woman, and then turned his attention to Oren. He located some rope and bound the big man, hand and foot.

Maggie sat at the table with her face buried in her hands as Cord entered the cabin through the open door. She looked up as he approached the table and her gaze crossed his. She had composed herself and was now more at ease.

"Thank you, Marshal. You saved my life." she stated sweetly.

Cord felt compelled to explain why this happened. "Ma'm, I have to tell you . . . it's my fault that this happened. I ran my mouth at Rudabaugh, telling him that your testimony would hang him. When he escaped, he thought that killing you would prevent that. If I hadn't said what I did, he probably would have just run and not bothered with you. Please accept my apology."

"You have nothing to apologize for. You did your duty and I'm still alive and nothing can change that. What will you do with that man now?"

"Well, for the present, I want to get you and him back to Cason's place. Rudabaugh's uncle and his men are on the loose so I don't want you out here alone. They may get the same idea that he got and come looking for you. Cason is bringing in a wounded man so we'll meet him there. If the Rudabaughs cause any trouble, we'll be better off there. Now then, do you have a buggy or a wagon?"

"Yes, there's a wagon in back of the barn. But why do you want it? I can ride."

"It's not you I'm concerned about. I'm not letting Rudabaugh near another horse. He'll light out at the first chance. He can ride in the back of the wagon, tied hand and foot, and that's the way he'll stay until I get him back to Denver and put him in a cell."

Maggie rose from the table. "I'll help you get things ready."

Chapter Ten

Macara was satisfied with a job well done. He had examined the wound in Grey Tumbley's shoulder and determined that the slug had passed through completely, surprisingly breaking no bones. Having cleaned and bandaged the area, and having administered some Laudanum for pain, he was now ready to help Tumbley navigate his way out of the brush to where the horses were now stationed, near Macara's cover during the firefight. With Tumbley's good arm wrapped around Macara's neck, Macara helped the man walk the distance to the horses. Weakness and the pain killer were now taking their toll on Tumbley and Macara realized that he would not be able to travel very fast. He helped Tumbley into the saddle, then mounted himself and set out for home.

Tumbley had not said a word in the time since Cord had left and Macara was actually content with that. He had nothing to say to this man. The aid that he provided was done because it was needed and that was the kind of man that Macara was. But conversing with a man who had just tried to kill him was more than Macara could muster.

They had not covered much ground when movement behind them caught Macara's attention. He glanced back to observe at least half a dozen men approaching at a gait just a tad more than a trot. Tumbley saw them also.

"Asa." he mumbled through the Laudanum.

"Aye." Macara agreed as his heart began to beat faster and his mind pictured all manner of dastardly deeds being done to him by these men for participating in Oren's arrest. Realizing he could not outrun them and being unwilling to leave his patient, Macara reined in. If this was to go badly for him, he would meet it head on. He turned to face the approaching riders.

At the head of the pack, Asa led the way to the waiting pair. He recognized both men and began wondering where Oren and the lawman were and what had transpired to put these two together on the trail. As the group came up to Macara and Tumbley, Asa called a halt.

"What the hell's going on?" Asa demanded. The question was directed to Tumbley.

Suddenly, Tumbley was talkative. "Oren escaped when I ambushed them. Cord went after Oren. This one fixed me up after Cord shot me."

Macara, in an effort to divert the conversation from the fact that Oren was after Maggie, chimed in: "I doubt that Cord can catch him. Oren had too long a head start. Cord will be heading back to my place. That's where we're going." He was counting on the Laudanum clouding Tumbley's brain and causing him to forget Oren's vow to kill Maggie. It worked because Tumbley said nothing about it.

Asa was puzzled but took both men at their words. "We'll all go back to your place." he told Macara, "I want another talk with that lawman."

Macara breathed a sigh of relief as he and Tumbley fell in with the group and continued the journey.

Cord completed hitching two of Maggie's horses to the wagon behind the barn while Maggie finished caring for the bay mare. When feeding and watering had been accomplished, she exited the barn. At the same time, Cord drove the team to the front of the barn and lowered the tailgate. He helped Maggie into the seat and entered the barn.

Oren was exactly where Cord had placed him and was still a neatly tied package. Cord squatted beside him and released the rope on his feet. Cord then rose and stepped back a few feet while drawing his revolver.

"Now then, get to your feet and walk outside." Cord ordered.

Oren struggled some and gave up. The bonds on his hands made it difficult. He was actually hoping to get Cord to release his hands, thus giving him a chance to attack Cord and turn the tables.

"I can't." Oren stated.

"You'll do it or I'll knock you out and drag you. One way or another, you're going outside."

Oren grumbled. He made another try and stopped short of getting his feet under him.

"Come on." Cord commanded.

Oren realized that he was not going to win at this and put extra effort into his struggle. Finally, with legs flailing, he gained a standing position. Cord waived the pistol toward the barn door opening in a silent order to move outside. Oren complied, walking somewhat unsteadily due to the lack of blood flow to his feet and the fact that his hands were pinned behind him.

Both men emerged from the barn and Cord directed Oren to the back of the wagon.

"Climb up." was Cord's next order.

Without protest, Oren backed up to the wagon and used his bound hands to pull his weight up so that his buttocks were in line with the wagon floor. He then scooted himself onto the wagon in a sitting position. Cord quickly looped the rope around Oren's feet and tied it off in a half hitch. Just as quickly, Cord put both hands under Oren's feet and lifted them, causing Oren to roll into the interior of the wagon. Cord's next move was to secure the tailgate and tie off the reins of his horse to the tailgate handle. With a pull on the wagon seat, Cord placed himself next to Maggie. He uncoiled the reins from the brake handle and slapped them smartly on the rumps of the team. "Hyahh! Get up there!" he called. The horses came to life and moved the wagon toward the knoll that led to Macara's store.

The store was completely quiet. The only movement was that of Cord's pack horse partaking of the salt lick at the fence of the small makeshift corral attached to the store. The skittish animal's head came up fast as a group of riders approached. Shying, the horse whinnied and retreated to the center of the corral seemingly for safety.

With Asa Rudabaugh in the lead, the riders entered the area and halted at the hitch rail in front of the store. "Macara." Asa called, "Where's the lawman?"

Macara dismounted as he spoke: "I've no idea. He just said he'd meet me back here. Didn't tell me when."

"Check the place out, boys. Make sure the lawman ain't here." Asa also dismounted as he spoke.

The riders came out of their saddles and fanned out, some heading for the small barn and others mounting the porch to the store. Their entry and search of both buildings went quickly and soon Asa was satisfied that Cord was not present on the scene.

Concerned for Tumbley, Macara approached Asa. "Do you mind if I get him inside so I can make him more comfortable?"

"Yeah, go ahead." was Asa's answer.

Macara helped the listless Tumbley out of the saddle and tried to half-carry him into the store. A bigger man, Tumbley proved too much for Macara to manage alone. "A tad o' help here, if you please?" Macara called to anyone who would listen. Two of the men gripped Tumbley and took him from Macara. They entered the store. "On the counter if you will." Macara instructed. The men placed Tumbley on his back on the counter and Macara placed a cushion fetched from his inventory under the man's head. Macara immediately set about rechecking Tumbley's wound.

"Is he all right?" Asa asked from the door.

Macara looked up. "He will be as long as this wound is cared for."

"Do it then." Asa seemed preoccupied and not as concerned for one of his own as he might be.

"I am. I am." Macara answered, equally preoccupied with his task.

Asa turned in the doorway and stepped across the porch to his horse. In the saddle holster hung a Sharps

Buffalo Gun, a formidable one shot killing machine. Across the back of the saddle beneath the cantle was a bandolier full of 45-70 rounds. Asa pulled the Sharps from its holster and released the strap securing the bandolier. He lifted the shell belt and threw it across his shoulder. Returning to the porch, he fetched a chair and sat with the rifle across his lap. His hand opened the breach and inserted a round inside. He then closed the breach and deposited two shells in the side pocket of his jacket. Asa was now ready for Cord.

Chapter Eleven

The wagon ride to Macara's was uncomfortable to say the least. The almost nonexistent suspension system was completely unforgiving, bouncing the passengers noticeably over the rough terrain. This caused Cord to limit the speed of travel to what he considered a crawl, for his concern for Maggie's comfort won out over his desire to see Oren quickly secured under lock and key. They didn't call this contraption a buck board for nothing, he thought, but it was all they had and they had to make due. Cord continually checked behind him, looking for signs of Asa's men and also to be certain that Oren was still safely deposited in the wagon bed. He was silent through the trip so far, saying only a polite no-thank-you to Maggie's offer of water from the canteen.

Maggie was equally quiet, reflecting on her now solitary life with Will gone, and what would become of her. She was a farmer's wife because Will was a farmer, but it was not her choice for a life alone. Keeping up the farm was her aim for the present, but this was not how she wanted the rest of her life to be. Not without Will. Without help, the place would quickly become too much for one person, and she could not expect Sam Luce and the others to continue helping her indefinitely. They had lives and places of their own to take care of. She had no money to hire help, so a decision would have to be made soon. Would she try to sell the farm and return to her family in New York? Would she try to make a life here where the people around her had become a second family? She had some skills: she could sew, she could cook . . . maybe she could move to a more populated area and open a shop of some kind. Maybe . . .

Having trailed off deeply in thought, Maggie suddenly caught herself staring at Cord. With that realization, she became strangely calm instead of embarrassed. This man exuded confidence and caring. In his presence, she felt completely safe and protected. This was the same way she had felt when she was with Will.

Eventually, Cord became aware of Maggie's stare. He turned his head toward her and smiled, putting her even more at ease. She smiled back.

Cord's attention to Maggie caused him to fail to direct the team around a bunch of rocks and the result was a series of bounces that nearly unseated them both. Now it was Cord who was embarrassed at his mistake and they both enjoyed a hearty laugh at the incident.

Cresting the hill that only yesterday had led Cord to Macara's place, Cord reined the team in. Experience told him that you don't just go on in to an area that could potentially be dangerous. You stop and survey. With Asa and his men on the prowl, anything was possible. Cord studied the scene, perceiving a figure in a chair on the porch. Closer observation convinced him that the figure was not Macara. He pointed at the figure and spoke to Maggie.

"That's Asa Rudabaugh down there. Not sure what's going on but it might be best if you wait here until I can find out."

Maggie observed the scene.

"I'd rather be with you." she said confidently. "I'd feel safer."

Cord stroked his chin. The thought of leaving Maggie alone on this slope did not appeal to him either, but he hesitated to put her in a possibly dangerous situation again. As he pondered, Maggie spoke up: "Are we going?"

Cord took a second, realizing that he had to take her with him, and formulated a quick plan. "Yes, but I want you to drive the team. I'll be in back with him. However this goes, I want a gun directly on him all the time."

"All right." she said.

Cord swung around on the seat and dropped onto the wagon bed. With his revolver trained on Oren, he nodded to Maggie. She picked up the reins and slapped them across the backs of the horses. The wagon proceeded down the slope slowly.

Asa had sat in the chair quietly for some time now, watching the country before him. He saw the wagon crest the hill and stop. Then, after several moments, it continued down the slope.

"Macara," Asa called over his shoulder, "get out here."

There was no reply. Asa called again. Macara appeared in the doorway. "Wagon coming." Asa stated and pointed to the oncoming conveyance.

Macara looked in the direction of Asa's finger and his blood suddenly ran cold. There was Maggie, with

Cord seated in the wagon bed, coming directly toward the store. He could not warn them or waive them off and here they were coming right into a trap.

Asa rose from the chair and placed the Sharps in line with Macara's middle. "Get yourself up against that post." he ordered. Macara backed up until his back was against the porch post. Asa kept the rifle leveled on Macara and continued to watch the approaching wagon.

While Cord's pistol was covering Oren, Cord was watching the scene on the porch unfold before him. That was Macara down there, under Asa's gun. This was going to become a stand-off that could go badly if it was not handled just right.

"When you get to the store," Cord said to Maggie, "jump down on the left side of the wagon and stay down." Maggie nodded nervously. Cord produced his knife and slit the bonds on Oren's ankles. Maggie continued to drive the team into the area of the store.

Asa's men had now joined him on the porch, three on each side of him. Asa still held Macara at bay as the wagon entered the scene. Maggie halted the team behind the saddle horses and let go of the reins. With one quick movement, she swung her legs over the side of the wagon and dropped to the ground keeping the wagon between her and the others.

Cord gripped Oren's shirt and rose to his feet, hauling Oren with him to a standing position. Cord's revolver immediately went to Oren's head.

"You let my nephew go, lawman." Asa ordered.

"Not a chance." Cord answered. He knew how this was going and decided that saying as little as possible, while maintaining a threatening position on Oren, was the best way to proceed.

Asa took an ominous step toward Macara. "I can cut him in half with one shot."

"And I can blow your nephew's head off." Cord stated calmly.

"You don't know me, Cord. I ain't got no compunction to killing you all. Now you let him go." Asa was becoming visibly agitated. Cord noted that Asa seemed to have a problem maintaining his control if a situation did not go exactly as he planned. This was good to know. It was now time to tip the balance.

"I'll fight him." Cord said concisely.

Asa heard Cord's words but, coming as they did from a completely different thought, they did not register on him. "What?"

"I said I'll fight him . . . hand to hand. I'm offering you a bargain. If he wins, he goes free. If I win, he goes with me to trial. But either way you let Macara go. He's done more to help you than hurt you. Your beef is with me, not him. What do you say, Asa, bargain?"

The offer took Asa completely by surprise. "You want to fight Oren?" he repeated incongruously, "You can't win at that. He'll grind you into the ground. I seen him do it."

"You let me worry about that." was Cord's reply, "Is it a bargain or not?"

"You lose, you're dead. You know that, right?"

"I know it."

"Oren," Asa called to his nephew, "you up for this?"

"I'm itchin' for it." Oren answered, a grin covering his face.

"All right, lawman, you got your bargain. Cut him loose and have at it."

Cord scaled the wagon tailgate and waived his revolver at Oren to follow him. When Oren was on the ground, Cord cut his bonds and stepped away from the man. At the side of the wagon, Cord released his gun belt and let it drop to the ground. Quickly, he removed Oren's Colt from his waistband and allowed that weapon to join his own.

Oren rubbed the blood back into his wrists and cracked another confident grin as Cord assumed the fighter's stance and made ready for the fight of his life.

Chapter Twelve

The two men circled each other threateningly.

Oren's face remained grinning with anticipation of the beating he had planned for Cord. This lawman had pushed him around and humiliated him for the last time. He was now going to pay and pay dearly. Oren would enjoy beating him to death.

Cord had not been involved in a fist fight for several years, but remembered now as he had then, the teachings of Sgt. Hedge. The good sergeant had been a prizefighter before he joined up, and was the instructor for the hand-to-hand combat classes that were given during Cord's training. Hedge had identified Cord as a natural fighter and had convinced him to take private lessons to develop his skills. The first lesson Hedge gave was to empty the mind of any other thoughts save for concentrating on sizing up the opponent and planning each blow based on the opponent's actions. Cord was doing that now as he carefully watched Oren.

Oren made a quick move designed to scare Cord. Cord did not react but continued to circle the big man. Immediately, Oren made a wide swing with his right fist, aimed at Cord's head. Cord saw the blow coming and had plenty of time to dodge it. As Oren swung, his balance shifted and he needed to take a step to keep from losing his footing. This caused him to leave his body unprotected and Cord heaved a short left into his kidney area. The jab continued Oren in the direction he was going and caused him to spin completely around.

Cord took note of the fact that Oren was not a very agile man. He lumbered and his balance was less than adequate. As Oren came back around to face him, Cord took a step toward him and landed several left jabs and a hefty right to his facial area. Oren staggered backwards, seemingly injured. Cord could not determine if the action was because he had hurt Oren or just knocked him off balance. Cord was not waiting to find out. He stepped in and pulled a left uppercut up from his knees that bruised Oren's chin, and immediately followed with a right hand chop that caught the side of Oren's face and opened a cut on his cheek. Oren descended to one knee and one hand, feigning injury. While Cord's blows hurt, they did not have the effect on Oren that he was making them out to have. His plan was to wear Cord out, to wind him, but he saw that this was not happening. Cord was as fresh as when he had started. Oren had to change plans.

Quickly, Oren scooped dirt with the hand on which he was leaning. With almost one move, his hand flung the dirt at Cord's face and his body sprang forward. As the dirt reached his face, Cord instinctively raised his hands in defense of the attack. Left unguarded, Cord was unable to protect himself from Oren's forward movement. Oren's shoulder sank squarely into Cord's chest. Cord bounded backwards, the wind knocked out of him, and sprawled on his back.

Oren regained his footing and moved to Cord. His left hand grabbed a handful of Cord's shirt and his right secured a grip on Cord's belt. With a great lunge, Oren lifted and heaved Cord's body toward the horses hitched to Maggie's wagon. Cord landed hard on his side and skidded on the ground.

Cord immediately rolled to his knees, knowing that his chances of continuing were nil if he could not get back on his feet. His hands went up to clear away the dirt that was sticking to his sweating face and now entering his eyes. He tried to breathe life back into himself and lost track of the time that this was taking. Suddenly, he realized that he had left himself completely unprotected as he felt his shirt being grabbed and his body being tossed forward, closer to the horses. He landed on his chest this time, dangerously close to the horses. The activity behind them caused the horses to shuffle nervously. A hoof came closer to Cord's head than he was comfortable with. While he was winded, his mind was still working and it forced his body to roll away from the horses. As he rolled he pulled his knees under him and forced his body up. Now he was on hands and knees and trying to crawl a safe distance away from the horses. And now Oren was in front of him and preparing to swing an open handed blow at him from above.

Oren heaved the blow at Cord with all his weight behind it. Cord rolled to avoid the hand and sent his body back toward the horses as Oren again lost balance and bounded off to the left. Oren's stumble gave Cord the opportunity to pull away from the horses and he managed to make it back to his feet and clear the dirt from his eyes. Now groggy, his stance faltering, Cord was defenseless when Oren drove forward and wrapped his arms around Cord's frame. Cord felt himself being lifted off the ground, trapped in Oren's increasingly restricting bear hug. Oren grunted more strength into the hug and Cord cried out as he felt his ribs compressing.

Cord searched frantically for a way out of this predicament. His mind worked quickly. While his body was trapped, his hands and arms were free. He brought both hands up to Oren's head and boxed the man's ears as hard as he could. He felt Oren falter but this did not work the way it was supposed to. Perhaps his aim was off or perhaps his strength had been sapped but boxing an opponent's ears should cause him enough discomfort to immobilize him. Another attempt also failed. Oren was beginning to squeeze harder. Cord was almost unable to breathe.

The eyes, Cord thought. Gouge his eyes. It was the only thing left to try that Cord was able to execute. Quickly, he grabbed hands full of Oren's long hair, brought it forward to use as a lever and jabbed his thumbs into Oren's eyes. Cord arched his back to provide even more leverage as he sank his thumbs into Oren's eyes with increasing pressure. A long grunt issued from his throat and he pushed even harder.

Oren screamed as the pressure on his eyes became unbearable. He felt as if his eyes were being driven into his head and the resultant pain overtook his every thought and action. His grip on Cord's body began slowly to relax, then, as the pain became all encompassing, he quickly let Cord loose. At that moment, Cord released his grip on Oren's eyes as he sank to the ground on shaky legs. Oren's hands immediately went to care for his injured eyes as Cord staggered around to regain the wind that he had been deprived of by the bear hug. But Cord's mind was still working. Don't let up, he thought. Stay on him! Finish him! Cord forced his body to function. On unsteady legs, he bounded forward and began landing stomach and upper body blows. Now unable to see very well, Oren was wide open and faltering.

Cord continued the barrage for several seconds, still unable to take Oren off his feet. Cord's punches, while telling, were not the caliber he desired because of his failing strength. He knew he needed more. Drawing a huge breath, he pulled back his right fist and threw it forward, throwing his body completely behind it. The blow hit Oren squarely in the chest, forcing him back and spinning him to his knees. The man was now coughing and gasping for breath.

Cord stepped in as he watched Oren struggle to regain a standing position. Cord had now discarded all thoughts of fairness. His only driving force was to whip this son of a bitch and end this. As Oren started to get up, Cord landed a chop to his head that sent Oren back to his hands and knees. Cord waited for Oren to fall but the big man did not. What the hell is holding him up?

Oren pulled himself to a position in which he was kneeling with his butt sitting on his heels. He was obviously trying again to get up. Cord moved in and took a handful of Oren's hair to lift his head. Holding on tightly for stabilization, Cord pushed a right cross forward that landed on Oren's nose. The blow drove the man's head back and Cord felt his grip pulled away, leaving some hair behind. Completely exhausted, Oren collapsed in a heap. Cord's hands went to his knees for support as his own exhaustion was now evident. He took several deep breaths to regain his wind as his mind attempted to convince his body that it was still functional. He stood straight and threw back his shoulders, then breathed a heavy sigh of relief.

Chapter Thirteen

Asa watched in awe and disbelief as Cord landed his final blow on Oren and Oren crumpled to the ground. This can't be happening. Nobody's never beaten Oren, just not nobody, not never! Cord ain't getting away with this. Never had no intention of honoring the bargain anyhow, but now Cord's got to pay dear for this. Don't kill him, just wing him. Make him die slow and painful. As he thought, Asa took the Sharps from covering Macara, swung it toward Cord and brought it up to firing position.

With the act of taking aim on Cord, Asa moved his eyes from Macara to Cord. In that instant, Macara saw his chance to act. As he sprang toward Asa, his hands outstretched and aiming for the rifle, Macara cried out, "Cord! Look out!" With the finish of the warning, Macara grabbed the rifle at the barrel and the breach and tried to wrest it from the bigger man's grip. From the scuffle the gun discharged into the air, but Asa held his ground and shoved the butt of the weapon at Macara. This act broke Macara's grip and Asa was able to extend the arc of the rifle, causing it to strike Macara's shoulder and reeling him off the porch to the ground.

At the sound of Macara's words, Cord turned to see the struggle. Realizing the danger that both he and Macara were in, his only thought was to get to his weapon. As Macara fell to the ground, Cord, seeing Asa attempting to reload the Sharps, took three wide strides toward the spot on which his gun and holster rested. He knew this would not be fast enough since Asa was now inserting another round into the rifle's breach, so Cord made a dive for his weapon. He landed on his chest and belly and skidded to a stop at his holster with both hands outstretched. His left hand grabbed the holster and his right hand pulled the pistol free almost in the same motion. He jammed his left boot heel into the ground and pushed himself into a roll that put him on his back. In one continuous motion, he spun and turned himself into a sitting position as Asa's rifle fired and placed a round into the dirt where, a second before, Cord's body had been.

Asa flipped the breach open to reload. Cord brought the revolver up to a two handed grip and leveled it on Asa. As Asa's hand came out of the jacket pocket with the next round, Cord cocked the pistol and found his mark on Asa's chest. His finger completed the trigger pull. One bullet exited the barrel and found its home deep in Asa's chest. Almost automatically, Cord fired another round which caught Asa slightly higher in the chest as the big man started to fall back, stopping his heart in mid-beat.

Asa's lifeless body was driven back against the building and slid to the floor of the porch. His hand let go of the rifle and the round. As they fell to the porch, Macara was bounding up the steps to scoop them up. He dropped the round in and closed the breach, then leveled the weapon on Asa's men who were crowded on the porch.

Cord pulled his feet under him, Indian style, and pushed himself to a standing position. His legs were still unsteady but he forced himself to move forward while leveling his weapon on the three men to Asa's left.

"You three, over there with the others." Cord ordered, using the revolver as a directional tool.

The three men were dumbfounded by the events that had just unfolded before them and did not immediately obey the command.

"Move!" Cord stated.

The men suddenly moved in unison, stepping across Asa's body and crowding in with the others.

Cord stepped to Macara's side. "Keep them covered, Deputy." Cord's words were more for the benefit of the men than for Macara.

"Absolutely, Marshal." Macara replied. He was smiling now.

More quietly, Cord asked, "Are you all right?"

"I'm as well as can be expected under the circumstances." Macara answered drolly. "And what about yourself?"

"Had better days." Cord said concisely. With that he moved to Asa's body and placed fingers of his left hand on the man's throat to feel for a pulse. There was none. It was as he expected. He had known when he fired the shots that he was shooting to kill and he had accomplished his purpose. But now the realization that he had just taken another's life was taking hold. He felt that familiar sick feeling in the pit of his stomach that he had known when incidents like this had necessitated similar actions. He asked himself if maybe he had aimed to wound the man . . . No this was the way it had to be. Asa would not have stopped until he was dead and trying to wound him may have caused more injuries. It had to end like this.

Cord rose and faced the six men who had ridden with Asa.

"Now then, listen up. Asa's dead. Up to now, as far as I know, all you've done is choose the wrong man to ride with. If you have done anything against the law, I can't prove it. So I'm giving you one chance. Ride out of here. Head north and don't stop until you cross into Canada. If I catch you back in these parts, it won't go well for you, I promise you that. Now, git!"

Almost as one, the body of men stepped gingerly between Cord and Macara and headed for their horses. There was some confusion as the men nervously sought out their own mounts and pulled themselves into the saddles.

Macara had turned to face the men but retained his position at the porch. Cord strode toward them purposefully.

"In case you're not sure, that's north." Cord informed them, pointing to the direction. "Now move out!"

The men pulled their reins and aimed their horses in the general direction of north. Heels and spurs dug into the animals' flanks as they struck out on their forced journey. Cord watched them as they rode off.

Macara stepped to the porch pillar where he had been held captive just minutes before and stood the Sharps rifle against it. As he turned back around, the scene that came into his view stopped him in his tracks.

"Oh, Lord have mercy." he uttered. Then he called loudly, "Maggie, no!"

Chapter Fourteen

Maggie Tremayne stood over Oren Rudabaugh's unconscious body with the Colt in both hands, staring at the man. Her thumb pulled back the hammer as she leveled it on the man.

Maggie had done exactly as she had been told when she drove the team up to the store. She had jumped off to the left and stayed put alongside the wagon while the standoff played out. Then there was the fight and she was not going to miss that, but she kept the wagon between herself and the action, moving to view it from a crouching position. She winced when it seemed to be going badly for Cord but was overjoyed when he finally won out. She reveled in the beating that Cord put on Oren and breathed a sigh of relief when Oren fell unconscious. When the shooting started, she found enough cover behind the front wheel to stay out of the line of fire. She even grabbed the team's reins to keep them from bolting and running off with her protection. Seeing Asa fall dead, she knew this was finally over.

As Cord directed Asa's men out of the area, Maggie ventured out from cover and around the rear of the wagon, ducking under the tied reins of Cord's saddle horse. Oren's body came into her view first and she was taken over by the realization that this terrible man who had taken her Will from her was still alive. He should be dead like the other one. He should pay the ultimate price for his deed. She looked around for the Colt, the gun that Oren had aimed at her with the intention of killing her when Cord had stopped him, and found it on the ground next to Cord's gun belt. He should be dead! This thought was all consuming in her mind. She stooped and picked up the Colt, regarding it as the instrument that would ultimately deal the final blow to this bastard who should never have been born. She took two steps to Oren's location and stood there holding the gun and staring at the man's battered face.

Maggie knew that this was fundamentally wrong but this was not a normal situation and this was not a normal man. He was not even a man; he was a wild animal that needed killing. She knew this would never bring Will back but this man needed to be dead. And she needed to know that his death was at her hand to pay him back for Will. This was the thought that permeated her brain as her thumb cocked the Colt's hammer. Tears welled in her eyes, clouding her view. With her left hand she wiped the tears away, and then placed the hand back on the pistol. Her hands shook and she was not certain if it was nervousness or anticipation of the thing she was about to do.

Macara's admonition shocked her back to reality and momentarily stopped her from proceeding. As Macara moved toward Maggie, Cord turned to view the scene.

"Darling lass, don't be even thinking about that." Macara said quickly as he approached her. "He's not worth the powder."

As he reached her he noted that the Colt was cocked and set to fire. He needed to keep talking, to distract her, to talk her out of this without that gun going off.

"You know Will wouldn't want this, not this way. Not putting you in harm's way. If you do this, things will never be the same. It'd be different if you were defending yourself, but to do it this way, in cold blood, that's not you." Macara was talking at breakneck speed, trying to keep Maggie's attention away from her task. "You'd be making yourself no better than him. And Marshal Cord would have to arrest you and I know he doesn't want to do that. And I know you don't want that. Maggie, darling, this man's going to hang for killing Will and that's a hundred times better than you killing him. And besides, he'll see it coming. Look at him now. He has no idea what's going on. If you kill him now he'll never know what hit him. And I'm sure you want him to know, to see it coming, to feel that rope around his neck, to know that his next breath will be his last. And it'll be done all legal and your testimony will seal his fate. Isn't that better than putting yourself in the same position? Maggie, think about what you're doing. I know you know it's wrong and I know you can't do it."

Maggie was sobbing now and her hands were shaking. Macara had visions of the gun going off even unintentionally by a twitching finger. He reached out and placed his hand on the Colt with his thumb between the cocked hammer and the cylinder, hoping to block the hammer from falling on a live round. As his grip tightened, Maggie relaxed her hold and Macara was able to pull the weapon from her hand. With the same motion, Maggie turned and fell into Macara's waiting arms, sobbing uncontrollably. Macara retained his grip on the pistol and raised his hand to move the weapon out of the way.

As Macara held Maggie, Cord moved in and took the Colt from Macara's hand. His thumb immediately lowered the hammer, taking the gun out of action.

Maggie took some time to calm herself, burying herself in Macara's embrace while she did. When she finally raised her head she looked across at Cord. He smiled that confident, reassuring smile that he had flashed in the wagon.

"I'm sorry, Marshal." Maggie said sheepishly.

"Don't be. Nothing happened." Cord replied. In those four words he was telling her that he felt her pain, that he understood her motives and that he was going to do nothing about the incident he had just witnessed.

Macara turned Maggie toward the store and started walking her. "Let's get you inside."

Cord stepped to the wagon and laid the Colt on the floor. He then crouched and picked up his gun belt, removed his revolver from his waistband and shoved it into the holster. While he strapped the gun belt on his waist, he moved to his mount and released the coil of rope from the saddle. A glance to Oren told him that the man was beginning to stir out of unconsciousness. He moved quickly to Oren and positioned him to be secured hand and foot. As Oren regained consciousness, Cord bound him with one length of rope that ran from holding his hands behind him to pulling his feet up behind him. Oren looked around at Cord as the last knot was tied.

"Trussed up like a steer ready for branding." Cord quipped, "And that's the way you'll stay till I get you back to Denver."

Macara stepped out of the back room as Cord entered the store.

"How is she?" Cord asked.

"It'll take some time but I think she'll be all right. Such a shame it is."

"Yes but it could have been a lot worse."

"Thanks to you it wasn't."

"And you. You make a hell of a deputy, Cason Macara."

Macara chuckled. "Ah, you know, I'm glad I'm not making it me life's work. What about Oren?"

"Tied up and dragged into the barn."

Cord moved his eyes to Grey Tumbley, still lying on the counter. "When do you think he'll be able to travel?"

"A week or two, I'd say. It's a clean wound and he's young enough to heal fast."

"Well then, if you'll have me, I'd like to stay here until I can get them both back to Denver. I'll work to earn my keep."

"Marshal Thomas Cord, there'll be no working for keep. You're a guest of this house. You not only have me undying gratitude, you have a standing invitation to partake of the Macara abode, humble as it is, for the rest of your natural life."

Smiling, Cord took Macara's extended hand and shook it vigorously, knowing full well that this would not be the last time their paths would cross.

Bob Giel

Macara suddenly changed the subject, looking up at Cord's head and remembering that the last time it was covered was when Tumbley started shooting at them and hit Cord's hat instead of his head. "Now, tell me, lad, might you be interested in securing a new hat from me fine sartorial inventory?"